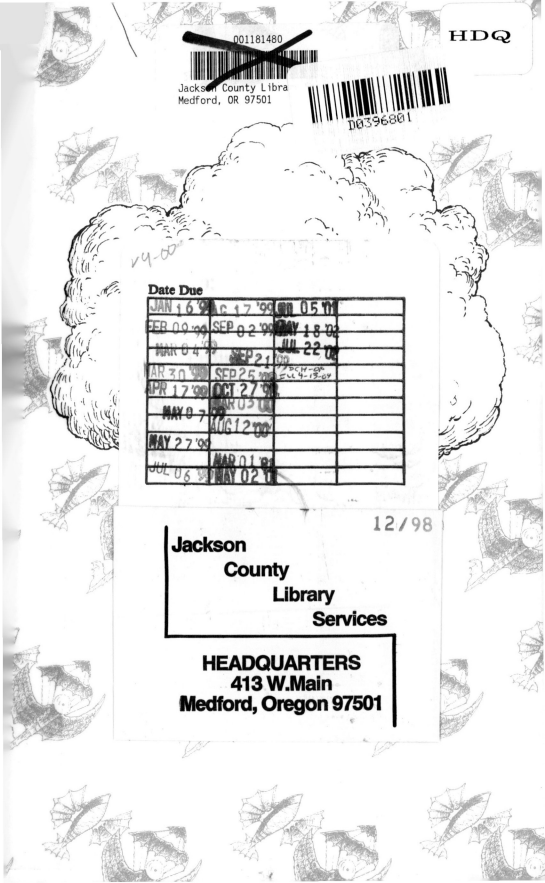

A H M E D

and the

O B L I V I O N

M A C H I N E S

Books by Ray Bradbury

Dandelion Wine
Dark Carnival
Death Is a Lonely Business
Driving Blind
Fahrenheit 451
The Golden Apples of the Sun and Other Stories
A Graveyard for Lunatics
Green Shadows, White Whale
The Halloween Tree
I Sing the Body Electric! and Other Stories
The Illustrated Man
Kaleidoscope
Long After Midnight
The Martian Chronicles
The Machineries of Joy
A Medicine for Melancholy and Other Stories
The October Country
Quicker Than the Eye
Something Wicked This Way Comes
The Stories of Ray Bradbury
The Toynbee Convector
When Elephants Last in the Dooryard Bloomed
Yestermorrow
Zen in the Art of Writing

A H M E D

and the

OBLIVION

MACHINES

A FABLE

Ray Bradbury

Illustrated by

CHRIS LANE

Avon Books   New York

Avon Books, Inc.
1350 Avenue of the Americas
New York, New York 10019

Text copyright © 1998 by Ray Bradbury
Illustrations copyright © 1998 by Chris Lane
Interior design by Kellan Peck
Visit our website at **http://www.AvonBooks.com**
ISBN: 0-380-97704-4

Library of Congress Cataloging in Publication Data:

Bradbury, Ray, 1920–
Ahmed and the oblivion machines : a fable / written by Ray Bradbury; illustrated by Chris Lane.—1st ed.
p.   cm.
I. Title.
PS3503.R167A68   1998   98-22746
813'.54—dc21   CIP

First Avon Books Printing: December 1998

AVON TRADEMARK REG. U.S. PAT. OFF. AND IN OTHER COUNTRIES, MARCA
REGISTRADA, HECHO EN U.S.A.

Printed in the U.S.A.

FIRST EDITION

QPM   10   9   8   7   6   5   4   3   2   1

With Love and Gratitude
to Chris Lane,
whose imaginative
sketches for
Tokyo Movie Shinsa's
LITTLE NEMO IN SLUMBERLAND
caused this book to be born.

A H M E D

and the

O B L I V I O N

M A C H I N E S

It was the night following the day when the seagull was seen over the desert that Ahmed, the son of Ahmed, fell from his camel and was lost as the caravan moved on into the dusk.

The gull had flown over at noon, coming from somewhere, going nowhere, circling back toward some invisible land that, they said, was rich with grass and water and had known nothing but water and grass for nine thousand years.

Looking up, Ahmed said:

"What does that bird seek? Here is no water and no grass, so where does it go?"

His father had answered:

"It was lost but now found again, returns to the sea from whence it came."

Ahmed, son of Ahmed, fell from his camel.

The gull circled a final time, crying.

"Oh," whispered Ahmed. "Shall we fly one day?"

"In another year," said his father, "but no one knows its name. Come. You must walk before you ride and ride before you fly. In the night, will your camel grow wings?"

And it was during that night that Ahmed stared at the sky and counted the stars until he was dizzy with counting. Then, drunk with light, he swayed as he inhaled the night wind. Crazed with delight at all that he saw in the heavens, he toppled and fell and was buried in the cooling sands. So, unseen by his father or the caravan of marching beasts, he was left to die among the dunes in the hours after midnight.

When Ahmed swam up through the sands, there were only the hoofprints of the great camels sifting away down the wind, at last gone, whispering.

I die, thought Ahmed. For what am I punished? Being only twelve, I do not recall any terrible crimes I committed. In another life, was I evil, a devil unseen and now discovered?

It was then that his foot scraped something beneath the shifting sands.

He hesitated, then fell to his knees to plunge his hands deep, as if searching for hidden silver or buried gold.

Something more than treasure rose to view as he swept the sand to let the night wind blow it away.

A strange face stared up at him, a bas-relief in bronze, the face of a nameless man or a buried myth, immense, grimacing underfoot, magnificent and serene.

"Oh, ancient god, whatever your name," whispered Ahmed. "Help this lost son of a good father, this evil boy who meant no harm but slept in school, ran errands slowly, did not pray from his heart, ignored his mother, and did not hold his family in great esteem. For all this I know I must suffer. But *here* in the midst of silence, at the desert's heart, where even the wind knows not my name? Must I die so young? Am I to be forgotten without having *been?*"

The bronze bas-relief face of the old god glared up at him as the sand hissed over its empty mouth.

Ahmed said, "What prayers must I offer, what sacrifice must I give, so that you, old one, may warm your eyes to see, your ears to hear, your mouth to speak?"

The ancient god said only night and time and wind in syllables that Ahmed understood not.

And so he wept.

Just as all men do not laugh or all women move alike, so all boys do not weep alike. It is a language that the ancient gods know. For the tears that fall come from the soul out of the eyes unto the earth.

And the tears of Ahmed rained upon the bronze bas-relief face of the ancient spirit and rinsed its shut lids so they trembled.

Ahmed did not see, but continued weeping,

And so he wept.

and his small rain touched the half-seen ears of the buried god and they opened to hear the night and the wind and the weeping, and the ears—*moved!*

But Ahmed did not see and his last tears watered the mouth of the god, to anoint the bronze tongue.

So at last the entire face was washed and shook to let bark a laugh so sharp that Ahmed, shocked, flailed back and cried:

"What!"

"Indeed, *what?*" said the gaped mouth of the god.

"Who are you?" cried Ahmed.

"Company in the desert night, friend to silence, companion to dusk, inheritor of the dawn," said the cold mouth. But the eyes were friendly, seeing Ahmed so young and afraid. "Boy, your name?"

"Ahmed of the caravans."

"And I? Shall I tell you *my* life?" asked the bronze face gazing up from the moonlit sands.

"Oh, *do!*"

"I am Gonn-Ben-Allah. Gonn the Magnificent. Keeper of the Ghosts of the lost names!"

"Can names be ghosts and lost?" Ahmed wiped his eyes to bend closer. "Great Gonn, how long were you buried here?"

"Hark," whispered the bronze mouth. "I have been to my own funeral ten thousand times your days."

"I cannot count that far."

"Nor should you," answered Gonn-Ben-Allah. "For I am found. Your tears move my eyes to see, my ears to hear, my mouth to speak long before the Sack of Rome or Caesar's death, back to the caves and the lions and the lack of fire. List! Would you save yet more of me and *all* of you?"

"I would!"

"Then no more tears! No more cries! With your robes, sweep off the dunes from the pavements of my limbs. Rouse Gonn the Great to the stars. My funeral bones bring forth, and

clothe them with your breath so that long before dawn, great Gonn will be reborn from your
sighs and shouts and prayers! *Begin!*''

And Ahmed rose and sighed and prayed and
shouted with joy and used his robes as broom
to sweep and quicken this newfound friend of
such a size the stars, seeing him, danced in their
pivots and shivered in their burning gyres.

And what Ahmed's breath did not move,
then his bare feet kicked away in the wind until
the great bronze torso burst free. And then the
snaking arms, the blunt fists, legs, and incredible
feet, so that the naked god was unclothed of
ancient dunes and lay under the burning gazes
of Aldebaran, Orion, and Alpha Centauri. Star-
light finished the revelation, even as Ahmed's
breath, a fount, went dry.

"I *am!*" cried Gonn-Ben-Allah.

And he lay there, three men wide and two
dozen tall, his torso a monument, his arms obe-
lisks, his legs cenotaphs, his face a noble half-
Sphinx, part sun god Ra, Arabian wits in fiery

eyes, and a storm of Allah's voice in his cavern mouth.

"I," said Gonn-Ben-Allah, *"am!"*

"Oh, you must have been a great god," said Ahmed.

"I strode the earth and shadowed continents. Now help me rise! Speak my hieroglyphs. The claw prints of the birds that from solstice to solstice touched my clay with prayers in codes, read and say!"

And Ahmed spoke to the sands:

"Now, Gonn of old, be young. Arise. Warm limbs, warm blood, warm heart, warm soul, warm breath. Come up, Gonn, up! Away from death!"

The great Gonn stirred and settled and then with a great shout shot into the heavens to sway above Ahmed, his limbs sunk deep as architectural pilings in the tidal sands. Set free, he laughed, for now it was a goodness beyond reckoning or word.

"There is reason, boy, why you stared and

fell to print the dust and waken me. I have waited an eternity for you, the keeper of the skies, the inheritor of the dream, the one who flies without flying."

And Gonn-Ben-Allah moved his arms to touch the horizons.

"The dream has stayed forever. Oh, the clouds, men have said. Oh, the stars and the wind that moves not stars but clouds. Oh, the storms that wander Earth to seize our breath. Oh, the lightnings we would borrow and hurricanes race. What jealous despairs we lie with nights and angered, know not flight!

"So you, boy, are the Storm Keeper."

And Gonn touched Ahmed's brow.

"Lead me with your dreams, which now must be remembered."

"How can I remember what is not?" Ahmed felt his eyes, his mouth, his ears.

"Step, walk, run. Then leap, bound, fly. . . ."

And as they watched, a great weather of darkness arose from that north from which all

And Gonn touched Ahmed's brow.

coldness comes, and that west which swallows the sun and that east which follows the death of the sun and darkens the sky. There were blizzards and hurricanes in the clouds and storms of lightning in its attics and the sounds of endless funerals lamenting as they fell off the edge of the world. The great blackness loomed over Ahmed and Gonn-Ben-Allah.

"What is that?" cried Ahmed.

"That," said Gonn, "is the Enemy."

"*Is* there such a thing?"

"One half of everything is the Enemy," said Gonn. "Just as one half of everything is the Saviour, the bright rememberer of noon."

"And what is the name of that Enemy?"

"Why, child, it is Time, and Time Again."

"But, oh, mighty Gonn, does Time have a shape? I did not know you could *see* Time."

"Once it happens, yes. Time has shapes and shadows to be seen. That, on the rim of the world, is Time to Be. A remembrance forward of things that will be erased, destroyed, if you do not grapple with it, seize it, shape it with your soul, sound it with your voice. Then Time becomes the companion to light and ceases to exist as the enemy of dreams.''

"It is so big," said Ahmed, "I'm afraid!"

"Yes," said Gonn, "for it's Time itself we fight, Time and the way the wind blows, Time and the way the sea moves to cover, hide, wipe away, erode, change. We fight to be born or not be born. The Unborn One is always there. If we can fire it with our souls, welcome it into living, its darkness will cease. I need you for that, boy, for your youngness is a strength, as your innocence is.

"When I fail, you must win.

"When I falter, you must race.

"When I sleep, you must fix your eyes on the stars to learn their journeys. At dawn the stars will have left their celestial roads, their Kings highways as faint breaths printed in the air. Before the dawn erases it, you must print it in your mind to show the way!"

"Can I do *that?*"

"And win a world and change men's destinies in clouds and flight? Yes! If you fly high you cannot escape Time, but you can pace it, and in the pacing, finish as its keeper."

"Still . . . I have never flown!"

"There was a day when you never *lived*. Would you have hid forever in your mother's womb?"

"Ah, no!"

"Well, then, before Time buries us, hear this—"

Gonn stretched his arms to the sky.

"I am the god of all the heavens and airs and winds that ever blew the earth since Time began, and all the dreams of men at night who wanted flight but lost their wings. So! I will summon windship ghost craft, to sail down Time to cross your sight and joy your heart! Now lo! hark, look, to truly *see!*"

Gonn in that instant exploded up till his nostrils plumed the clouds to crack the sky:

"Let all the kite machines arise, let storms of

Time erupt to summon ghosts. Hear me, all you north winds that haunt the lands. All the gales that rise from the south to fire summer around the globe. Hear me, east and west winds, full of flimsy skeletons of impossible machines! Hear!''

Then Gonn the Magnificent gestured like a player of harps.

''Ahmed, who knows the future but does not know he knows! Run, jump, fly!''

And Ahmed ran, jumped, and then . . .

''I fly!'' gasped Ahmed.

''Indeed!'' Gonn wove his fingers to pull the strings of this puppet. ''But if we go north we miss what lies south. If we go west we shun the mysteries of the east. Only if we fly in *all* directions can we find what we seek. Wings, boy. Wings!''

Ahmed spun about, crazed and alarmed. ''But if we fly in all directions, how can we arrive *somewhere*? Are there no maps?''

''Only those written in your blood.''

''But,'' cried Ahmed, ''oh, god of confusions, where are we going?''

"I fly!" gasped Ahmed.

"Yestermorrow!"

"Yestermorrow!?"

"That which once *was* and that which will *be!* Locked in your heart, remembrances of lost time. Ghosts buried in the past. Ghosts buried to be awakened, in the future."

"In what year?" cried Ahmed, upside down.

"Any year; there are no such things as years. Men made up the names of years to keep track. Ask not the year."

"What day, then, and what hour?" Ahmed felt the words spun from his mouth.

"Clocks are machines that pretend at Time. There is only the rising and the setting of the sun. There are no such things as weeks and months and hours. Say only that we move in space."

"Toward what once *was?* Toward what one day will *be?*"

"Clever boy. That is all that Time truly is. The past we try to recall, or the future which is just as impossible and unseen!"

"We move both ways, then?"

"Truly, that is our motion. Witness!"

And Ahmed looked down and saw:

A vast sea of sand which lay shore upon shore upon shore, surfing itself, falling to lay itself out in shuffles of white, flourishes of stone and rock and pebble that had gone through the granary of the sea a million years ago, before the sea pulled back to leave this endless desert and men to stake their tents and drive their camels and raise the walls of cities. But now it was all stillness, a great blanket of silent dunes from which, here or there, soft liftings of sandbanks appeared as if, beneath the surface, the limbs and torsos of buried gods were hid. And here and there, half seen, the covered, the masked face of an ancient worshipper of the turning stars and the passing wind and the unseen years sifting like the merest veil of sandstorm, here a nose about to break through, there a chin waiting to tremble, a mouth to speak, though choked with dust. And beneath yet another dune, a blunt forehead, a brow lost in its own past, gone lunatic with silence.

Beneath the surface . . . buried gods were hid.

"Oh," gasped Ahmed, flailing his arms in panic to swim the air, "what is buried here? A city long dead or a city as yet unbirthed, waiting to be born?"

"Both!"

"How can that be?" Ahmed sank, then rose, exclaiming, "How *so?*"

"One is lost memory. The second is remembered forward beyond tomorrow. We call that 'dream.' To recall rebuilds the past. To imagine builds the future. One city fits within the other. Life sits in death. Our futures rise from the grave. Two cities. One unreal because it has vanished. The other unreal because it rests in that living grave between a sleeper's ears. The past exists because it once was real. The future exists because we *need* it to be real. Look upon this phantom scene. Tell me, what is lost, what is yet to be found? What left behind, what far ahead? Are they not twins? Is not the future a mirror reflecting the past, aching to be born? Be silent. Witness. Then speak!"

Ahmed hovered and stared, stared and blinked, scanned this wasteland lit by sunrise a thousand years past or sunset in a calendar as yet unprinted. And then he said:

"I feel . . . many men, many women lost under the sand, coming and going with their sons and daughters. I feel great stones. Is this a graveyard, then, with catacombs and tombs along this dry sea? Catacombs, tombs, mummies, death!" shouted Ahmed, wrapped in ice, drowning in cold winds. "Death!"

"No!" cried Gonn, reaching out to seize the boy. "Cellars. Library cellars to be filled with thoughts, fancies, impossible futures brought to life!"

"Death!" Ahmed cried, and then, looking to the far countries of sand where untouchable beasts walked away and away from him, "Father!"

"Do not cry out to fathers," said Gonn. "Cry out to yourself to be saved."

"Death!" And Ahmed, in one mournful cry, fell.

And as he fell, swift, diminished, exhaled, punctured like a vast aerial balloon, so fell Gonn, moaning, into the dunes. Where he struck like a mighty meteor, only a crater of dust showed his ruin, even as Ahmed, similarly fallen, did not sink to dust but sprawled, stunned, to pick himself up under an empty sky and an empty procession of moonlit dunes.

"Gonn!" he said.

No answer.

"Gonn!" he bleated.

Silence.

The merest suction of sand dimpled in, murmuring, near his cheek.

"See," said a hollow whisper. "What?" said the lost voice. "You . . ." More sand sank upon itself. ". . . have done?" Fading: "I die. You . . . have . . . killed . . . me."

"No!" Ahmed clutched at the funneling hole in the dune. "Come back, Gonn. I need you!"

"No . . ." came the voice beneath the sand, "not me . . ."

Ahmed dug frantically and groped and dug only sand and air.

"Gonn. Where are you? Rise."

"Your father weighs me down."

"He can't. He mustn't!"

"He is your past. You must be your future. Put him away. Remove him from my limbs, my heart, my head!"

"How, how??!!" Ahmed dug deeper to nothing and more nothing.

"Avert your gaze. Look not to horizons with blood of your heart and beasts that stay fastened to the earth. Dance upon my grave."

"What?"

"Dance. No more tears or I am flooded as well as brought to slaughter. I am almost gone. Dance."

And wiping his eyes and looking not at the horizon where his to-be-forgotten father lived, Ahmed danced.

And beneath the cold dune long after midnight he felt a stir, a mighty commotion as if a god's heart had started up.

"Dance upon my grave."

And he danced more.

"Sing . . ." said the mighty whisper.

And Ahmed not only danced to kick away the dust, but sang as if from the highest minaret in a great land, and the large heart hidden grew larger and banged itself to life.

And if for an instant Ahmed lifted his gaze to search the land, prepared to cry out, then the huge heart slackened and the sand froze, so that he fixed his gaze only on his feet, which moved and leaped and pummeled the hidden heart as he shouted wild words of love to exhume, to revive, to prolong, to rouse.

"Yes!" came the mighty whisper, the buried voice. "Ah, yes, son of my heart and life, he who dances to waken fire and know no limits to the sky or earth. Dance, sing, dance, there!"

And with this last explosion, the sands were riven and, like a mountain, a storm, a celebratory rocket, Gonn was rebirthed, soared, and lifted Ahmed with him.

Among the clouds, both laughed and

Ahmed's tears were tears of relief and joy, and so accepted, as Gonn hurled questions:

"Does the caravan exist?"

"No," said Ahmed.

"Do you see it anywhere?"

"No," replied Ahmed.

"And the men of that long march?"

"Are gone," Ahmed responded.

"And someone's father with them?"

"And that father with them."

"Which means this present cannot blind you to the future? Good," said this great mouth in this great head on this great body. "See *more!* Be a proper gravedigger. Let your soul instruct your heart, let your heart speak to your tongue. Exhale. Celebrate. Shout!"

Ahmed inhaled deeply of the high sweet clear-water air.

"Let go!" said the huge mouth, almost engulfing him.

Ahmed exploded out all of that incredible air.

And the dry sea below, the ocean tide of shore on shore of dunes shouldering dunes, shivered.

"Again!"

Ahmed exhaled.

And the sand swarmed up like locust flights.

And what lay beneath was revealed.

"Great Gonn." Ahmed was panicked into delight. "Have I done *this?*"

"All this has Ahmed done."

And below were not cities buried stone on stone, but marble cliffs from which one day those towns would be built, and atop the cliffs were blood, bone, and webbed creatures that flung themselves out to kite-sail like scythes to cut the wind; grinning reptiles with oiled, unsavory smiles.

"How terrible!" Ahmed flinched and raised his hands to shield his face. "What made them?"

"Why, the One God whose nightmare gave them birth."

"How are they called?"

"Don't call, they might *come*. Nameless they were for a million beast generations, until on museum walls they were given names. But these bony kites were shut like fans long before you woke in the womb. Their wingprint smiles are fixed in stone below the cliffs. No ape or man ever witnessed their flight. Only their hieroglyph smiles remain. Quick!"

And Gonn and Ahmed fled upward in a midnight explosion of bats fired from caves, flung out to feed on winds of locust and moth and mosquito.

And the sky was empty now as trees arose and batwing squirrels capered across the moon.

"Flight," whispered Gonn. "And flight again. High journeys to drive men mad with envy when at last man came. Flight."

"Flight," said Ahmed.

And then the mighty friend to Ahmed exhaled, as did the boy, and more sand sifted away on a shoreline as vast as the eternal sky to reveal streets and towns and people fixed like statues there, stranded as the dry sea vanished and they all looked to the cliffs where once the dread kites soared, but now as the sun rose in the midst of darkness a man and his son, clothed in golden feathers embedded in bright wax, stood atiptoe on the cliff's rim.

"Higher," cried Ahmed, "I must *see!*"

And Gonn-Ben-Allah spun higher to see the man and his son with golden wings leap, thrust, fly off the cliff, with the son mounting higher and higher as the old man, alarmed, tried to shout him down. But the noon sun fired his wings to melt the wax to golden tears which dripped from wrist, elbow, and arm. And he fell like a stone from the sky.

"Catch him!" Ahmed exclaimed.

"I cannot."

"You are a god who can do anything."

"And he is a mortal who must *try everything.*"

And the flier with golden wings struck the sea and sank in bright rings, and the sea was silent as the sun died and the moon returned.

. . . And his son with golden wings leap, thrust, fly . . .

"How terrible!" Ahmed exclaimed.

"Oh, how brave," said Gonn.

They circled to see the father hover to mourn above the quiet surf.

"Did," said Ahmed, "all this truly *happen?* It must be so."

"Then it is so."

"Though his wings melted and he fell?"

"Even so. There is never failure in trying. *Not* to try is the *greater* death."

"But what does it *mean?*"

"It means," said Gonn-Ben-Allah, "that you *must* toss feathers in the wind and guess their directions to all points of the heart's compass. It means you must jump off cliffs and build your wings on the way down!"

"And *fall?* And never fear?"

"Fear, yes, but brave beyond fear."

"That is a big thing for a boy."

"Grow with its bigness, let it burst your skin to let forth—lo!—the butterfly. Quick!"

And they raced the windstream over the earth and beheld:

An airship made up of thistles, pollen, milk-weed, a craft so light it trembled at a child's breath. Its masts and spars were immense reeds that bent with the weight of ghost dandelions. The sails were cobweb and swamp-mist and its ship's captain a weightless mummy of tobacco weed and autumn leaf that rustled even as the sails above him shuffled the storm wind. An acre of ship with an ounce of cargo. Sneeze! Ahmed did! And it vanished in flakes.

As they raced the windstream again to find:

A balloon as ripe as a peach and as tall as ten acrobats, filled with hot wind from a basket of fire slung beneath its gulping mouth, inhaling flame, ascending with its passengers—a rooster, and a dog barking at the moon, and two men waving at an audience sea below.

And a woman in a strange dress and bonnet, laughing in the clouds as her balloon caught fire and fell, shrieking.

"No!" cried Ahmed.

"Refuse no sight. People fall but to rise

again!'' whispered the Great God of Time and Storms. ''Open your eyes!''

Ahmed blinked and saw the curve of earth where a kite was flung up in a cloud stream. In a vast bamboo frame with silk banners, like a spider caught in its bright web, a man struggled to tilt the kite. Ambling over and down with the tidal winds, he soared up like a wild exclamation point.

''I fly,'' he cried, ''I fly!''

And knew the joy of being high above a world of night.

But hearing his high laughter at conquering hills of cloud and storm, a hundred men did mutter in their sleep, and shout confusions to deny his high trajectory. Hid from his upward truth, slammed their eyes shut, erased his flight, as if it never were, and with empty guns and empty minds fired the sky.

Even as a blizzard of arrows rose to pierce his triumph of paper and silk, the Chinese emperor's symbol on each dart. The soaring man was struck, pinned to a cloud, as his last shout "I fly" became "die, I die," and fell as if lightning had torn his silks. Where he had been was air and emptiness.

He was gone as if he had never been. Gunshot by men who refused his sight, destroyed by doubt and envy, the flier had let go his joy, let loose the wings from remembered birds, and fallen.

And suddenly, as if pinned against the sky himself, Ahmed shook like a paper toy.

Gonn-Ben-Allah said, "Have you no words?"

"No words for what I have seen," mourned the boy. "Oh, mighty one, how I wish for one glimpse of my father and my camel."

"Patience. You must be strong without that medicine and so survive to give me birth. . . ."

Ahmed was astonished. "But you are already *born!* I speak to you. You are *real.*"

"Only the promise of the real, the possibility of birth."

"But I speak, you *answer!*"

"Do you not talk in your sleep?"

"Yes, but—"

"Well, then. Without *you*, I will never be truly born. Without *me*, you will be the walking dead. Are you strong enough to birth a god?"

"If gods can be born of boys, then yes. And now?" He gazed up into the immense bronze face of the half-dreamt deity. "What?"

"This!" cried Gonn-Ben-Allah.

And below, along the endless seacoast of dead sand, a volcano of buildings erupted.

"What are *those?*" Ahmed wondered.

"Men who flew in stone, marble, and clay, who dreamed wings but settled for arches and beams, palaces and pyramids, each mightier than the last, destined to fly in place, then fall to dust. Because they could not stretch high, loom free, they chose the lower road, which, still seen, made their hearts grow wings in their breasts and made their blood rise heavenward with that strange sound joy makes, laughing to see such buildings as opened their windows to set their souls free.

"But that was not true flight, for their feet were caught in clay. Even on those towers, where wings might soar, all hope died and men sank back to dreaming.

"So behold a pyramid here, a Great Wall beyond. Perches from which boys, grown men, might leap to die, hoping for wings."

And the winds blew and the sands recovered the cities and Ahmed and Gonn sailed on.

To see men who wove carpets and hurled them with shouts: "Rise!" But the carpets floundered and fell.

And saw a collector of butterflies sew up a thousand small bright wings, a bloom of spring flight which, as he stepped from his roof, exploded at his first shout of joy and last shout of silence.

And saw a thousand umbrellas fall as Earth's gravity flattened a mad boy in summer grass.

And saw yet other machines, all fans and whirligigs and hummingbird flickerings, driven before the rain, dissolved into a mindless sea.

"I see!" Ahmed exclaimed.

"See more. From all you have found this night, call forth each foundling toy! Fill the sky, then burn their shadows in your head, so as never to be lost. Now!"

"Yes!" Ahmed spun to shout: "All you ghosts of Forever, rise! Who *says*?"

"Ahmed," whispered Gonn.

"Ahmed!" echoed the boy.

"Of the Oblivion Machines."

Ahmed hesitated, then: "Of the Oblivion Machines!"

And where before had been a hundred, now ten thousand wasp, dragonfly, reptile shapes flicker-lit the moon. And all about was a sound on sound of rivers, then Amazons, then mighty *oceans* of wings.

And Ahmed slapped his hand and all the heavens were thunderclaps of applause with no lightning, drumshots of clamor: bone-breaking eruptions of boys and men, woven skeletons across the clouds.

"Of the Oblivion Machines"

"Silence!" commanded Ahmed, guessing from the silent mouth of Gonn what to shout. "Hold still!"

And the thunder died and the half-seen, half-guessed phantoms were transfixed against a sky half sight of moon, half glimpse of sun.

"Now," whispered Gonn. "In all the beds and all the rooms of the world."

"In all the beds," recited Ahmed. "In all the world's rooms, go to your windows to see what *must* be seen!"

And below now lay all the cities and towns of sleeping dreamers.

"Wake!" cried Ahmed with Gonn's voice. "Wake while the sky is full of shapes. See! Find!"

"Gods, oh, fellow gods," cried Gonn suddenly, gasping, clutching his throat, his chest, feeling his wrists, his elbows and arms. "I fall, oh, brother gods, I falter, I will fall!"

And great Gonn snatched at the wind with his fingers, his hands, beat his arms up and down, churned the clouds with frantic legs, glancing with fear down at the sleeping cities.

"They have buried me, killed me a thousand times to fit in a thousand tombs with no names."

"Who?" cried Ahmed.

"The dreamers that do not dream, the dreamers that do not do. The doubters who kill the dream. The walking dead who see birdless skies and shipless seas and horseless highways with not a carriage, not a wheel. Those who bed early and rise late and sleep at noon and eat figs and drink wine and cherish only flesh. They, oh, they, they, them!"

Ahmed stared down, blinking wildly, trying to find what was described.

"But they're not doing anything! They're all asleep."

"Their silence stops my ears."

"They're snoring!"

"They breathe in but not out. They take air and give nothing! I die of it!"

And Ahmed saw the cause:

The cities slept and the dust buried the sleepers, who were as dust, and the dream died in them, the bones of dreams with no flesh, with no men to man them, no pilots to steer and guide them, no flesh for the bones of the Oblivion Machines. They were ghost kites, ruins in the sky destined to tatter and snow into dinosaur graves and elephant tombyards.

No man stirred.

"How can they hurt you, Gonn? They're not even *moving*."

"They play at Statues and would make me one!"

"They don't know you *exist!*"

"Truth! And their not knowing further diminishes me. Witness, I lose substance, flesh, and weight. I melt with disbelief."

And as Ahmed watched, this, too, was true.

Great Gonn, as if burned in a sluice of invisible flame, flailed out arms and legs that were dwindling to shank and marrow. Where vast balcony chest was, now ribs emerged. His chin sharpened to a sword, his nose a razor, his lips a waxen grin over death's-head teeth.

"Oh, great Gonn, stop!" Ahmed cried.

"I am a tombyard god. Only living flesh and blood and human dream can help. I, a whale, am now carp and minnowed fingerling. Who will save me?"

"Gonn, oh, Gonn!" The boy writhed to find the words. "Me!"

"You!?" shouted Gonn. "Have you learned the first lesson well?"

"Yes!" yelled Ahmed.

At which Gonn's face suffused with pinks and crimson fires and his diminishment ceased and his bones, his ribs, sank back in refurbished skin.

"How *dare* you!"

"Because I'm the only one *awake!* Do you see anyone *else?* I'm up here, Gonn, but they don't know *I* am here, *either!* Oh, blast them, Gonn, and *burn* the fools!"

And Gonn gained further weight. His lips hid his skull's teeth. His sunken eyes blossomed in fuller lids.

"Would you be a god, then, like Gonn, and forgotten and maybe dead before your time?"

"Why not?"

"Courageous boy."

"No, only mad!"

"Madness *is* courage! Your madness is a meal. Fatten me!"

The boy seized Gonn's hand. Gonn, a balloon, ascended.

Ahmed stared at his hand gripped in the fist of this sick deity made well.

"It works!"

"Aye!" laughed Gonn. "Prayer builds a mighty fortress upon air!"

"I *never* pray!"

"You *do!* He who speaks tomorrows prays!"

Ahmed scanned the sullen dunes and sunken ruins.

"Teach me more, Gonn. How to fly higher and longer and swifter so—"

"So?"

"I can fly over these ruins and towns and shout."

"To waken the dead?"

"Some *must* hear, mustn't they? Some will wake, yes? If I keep on shouting."

"A lifetime of shouting? To tell them what?"

"Look here. How high. How great. What joy. You, *too!*"

"The simplest songs are best. You have sung one. So now you are Gonn the insignificant on his way to being son of Gonn, and a mighty god."

"I just want the *world* to be mighty!"

"Unselfishness; that earns you another thousand years in Paradise."

"Not Paradise! I just want people out of bed. And I want to be with you, Gonn, *forever!*"

"No! For now that he has a son, Gonn must partake of Time. Take me back to where you wept me awake. Bury me. This time with *happy* tears."

"Oh, Gonn, don't be dead!"

"Ah," laughed the god. "I will not die! In the moment of your birth, child, did you not know that my symbol was stamped on your brow?"

"Here?" Ahmed touched his brow.

"My immense thumbprint, which hides in the maze of your secret self. What you can *be*! That thumbprint is all your future life, dream, and doing if you act. But in the hour of birth, that great thumbprint vanished, sank down into your brow to hide unseen—"

"Unless?"

"You seek a lifetime's days for it, in mirrors where you drink deeply to find the you that is truly you, and be a being born into this earth to *become*."

"And what if I do not find my brow's thumbprint?"

"You need but look each day to find a line; at dark, another line; until, full grown, you gaze into your glass and *all* is there. Is your brow large enough to share space? Is there room for my body, arms, legs, head, and clamorous mouth in that skull? Permission to hide?"

"Oh, Gonn." The boy laughed. "Welcome!"

"Then hide me so I'll live, child, behind your eyes. Quick, a few last lessons. So!"

And hand in hand through clouds and sky, Gonn shadowed the tombyard cities and avenues of dust, and gave the boy more flesh and mightier if unseen wings, and Ahmed cried down at the vanished places.

"I'll be back! I won't let you rest!"

And fly they did until, exhausted, they simmered down to the volcanic pit where Gonn had ascended to shadow the heavens.

"The sun sets. Before it does, you will find your caravan, child."

"But I am lost!"

"Once, yes, some hours ago. But fly high enough, look long, and there it will be."

"I can't leave you here," the boy wailed.

"Come back many years from now when, as

a man, you have invented air and swum in clouds and moved the world from place to place in your own Oblivion Machine. And dig and find your great Gonn's golden face, as it was just at dawn this day, and fix it as medallion to your lightning device and *we* shall fly again. Done, Ahmed?"

"Done!"

"Now weep to wet the sand and lubricate my way."

And Ahmed loosed his final tears, which did just that.

And Gonn, with a mighty laugh and winking both his golden eyes, sank down and down like a massive spike driven by a last blow of light, until his own wet eyes were gone and then his brow and then his windblown hair and the sand settled, blowing with the breeze of dusk.

Ahmed wiped his eyes, searching the sky.

"I've forgotten already."

"No," came the whisper from the sand. "First left."

Ahmed lifted his left arm.

"Now right."

Ahmed lifted his right arm.

"Now left and right, right and left, up, down, down, up, left, right. So! *Ah!*"

And Ahmed flew.

And, exhaling, Ahmed thrust himself across a desert span to be gentled down where the caravan lay asleep with beasts and where his father, awake and grieving for his lost son, plunged from his tent to stumble in surprise upon that very son and not know him in the dark and, knowing him, fall to his knees and crush Ahmed with weeping and praise God who is the One God.

"Son, oh, my son, where have you been?"

"I flew, Father. See. Above to the north. Those clouds. I lived there a while. There were a thousand ships around me in the air that crossed the moon. I was lost, but he led the way across the night."

"*He?*"

Ahmed thrust himself across a desert . . .
where the caravan lay asleep . . .

"He whose feet drink of the earth and whose head knows the sky. And you cannot see him, Father, for he is hidden." Ahmed touched his brow. "Do you not see the smallest print of a great thumb?"

Ahmed's father looked deep into his son's face and saw there the sky and the night and the far traveling.

"Praise Allah," he said.

"Oh, Father," said Ahmed. "If one night I should again fall from the caravan, might I land on a marble floor?"

"Marble?" The father shut his eyes and thought. "In a northern place where scholars live and where teachers profess and professors teach? Teach what?"

"The air, Father, the winds, and, perhaps, the stars."

The father gazed into his son's face. "It must be so."

And among the sleeping camels in his tent Ahmed was laid to rest and during the time before dawn called out in his sleep.

"Gonn?"

"Yes?" A whisper.

"Are you still with me?"

"Always and forever, boy. As long as you loom my shadows between your ears. Paint pictures on the inner sides of sight so never to be alone. Speak, and I manifest. Whisper, and I shuttle and weave. Call, and I am the companion of light. *See!*"

And within his brow, indeed, Ahmed beheld heaven swarmed with circling craft shaped of gold leaf and silver foil and silks the color of the moon.

"Oh, Gonn," whispered the boy.

"Say not my name. I have another now!" Fading. "Ahmed. Call me that."

"Ahmed?!"

Silence. A dawn wind.

Sleep. And in his sleep, Ahmed saw himself grown and in a great craft with rotary blades whose rushing fans stirred the hot sands away and away until he stared down to see:

Ahmed saw himself grown and in a great craft . . .

There in the sand a face of beaten gold, with the eyes of a god and the smile of a reborn child.

And the medallion was plucked from the sand and placed as emblem on his craft, and Ahmed flew away to the future.

As the sand, emptied of treasure, cooled, and the future arrived.